4/21

TRULY
tyler

TERRI LIBENSON

BALZER + BRAY
An Imprint of HarperCollins*Publishers*

Balzer + Bray is an imprint of HarperCollins Publishers.

Truly Tyler
Copyright © 2021 by Terri Libenson

Library of Congress Control Number: 2021931993
ISBN 978-0-06-289457-1 (trade)
ISBN 978-0-06-289456-4 (pbk.)
ISBN 978-0-06-311673-3 (special edition)
ISBN 978-0-06-311447-0 (special edition)
ISBN 978-0-06-311909-3 (special edition)
ISBN 978-0-06-309512-0 (special edition)
ISBN 978-0-06-311782-2 (special edition)

Typography by Terri Libenson and Laura Mock
21 22 23 24 25 PC/LSCC 10 9 8 7 6 5 4 3 2 1
❖
First Edition

To my mom, dad, and siblings Brad and Tina,
who were always cool with my love of comics.
(Brad, sorry for stealing your MAD Magazines.)

PROLOGUE

Sometimes I look around the cafeteria at lunch and wonder why everything is set up the way it is. Why the jocks sit near the front. And the Science Club kids sit in back. And the manga kids sit near the ice cream freezer. Why the volleyball team sits near the windows and the orchestra kids sit near the tray conveyor belt. Which, by the way, is kinda unfortunate.

blend of mushy peas, pizza dregs, and b.o.

I guess I'm lucky I'm into sports. Otherwise I might end up here:

It's not that my friends aren't smart, too. Okay, maybe not smart-smart. But there are times I think . . .

I doubt anyone else in my group thinks about this stuff. They probably don't see the point of being friends with anyone else. Not sure if that's good or bad.

All I know is, more and more, I kinda like getting to know different kinds of people.

art and manga club kids

I just wish . . .

. . . we weren't so divided.

TYLER

I'm sure lots of kids are sad when winter break is over. Like the ones who get picked on at school. Or the kids who go away with their families to Florida and have to come back to the cold and snow. Even the ones who stay home during break and do regular stuff (playing video games, watching movies) probably hate it when they return to school.

Me? I'm the opposite. I love going back. I know that sounds weird, but if you lived in my house, you'd understand. It's not exactly an amusement park.

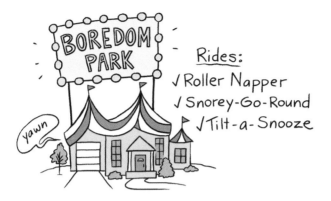

Things haven't been the same since Zach—that's my big brother—went to high school. Now he always goes out with friends or to practice or work. When he is home, he stays in his room and plays bass guitar or talks to his girlfriend. Zach stopped playing Fortnite with me a while ago.

And all my mom wants to do—when she's home—is play Scrabble.

But I understand Zach. If I had a driver's license and my own car (bought with money from a tae kwon do assistant's job), I'd be gone, too. But that's not happening for:

I did try to make the most of being home. I played video games and pickup basketball at the Y with Anthony Randall and Joe Lungo the first week. But a huge blizzard kept us home the rest of break. All I did was practice my trumpet and draw.

I did get special permission (think: begging), to go to Anthony's house for Christmas Eve. He's my best friend (don't tell Joe!).

Anthony and I have known each other since preschool. I've only known Joe since last year when we came to Lakefront Middle from different elementary schools. We were put on the same team in sixth grade (our school is so big, they divide the classes into "teams"), and that's when we became friends.

Anyway, back to Christmas Eve, which was awesome. Anthony's parents made this whole spread, and nothing was from a frozen bag. Anthony has two little two sisters who talked nonstop and fought over the butter rolls. His huge shaggy dog, Phineas, was under the table the whole time, taking turns licking crumbs and my big toe.

crumbs and sock-covered toe:
tied for deliciousness

His dad asked me lots of questions, which totally mortified Anthony but didn't bother me. My dad usually asks me the same two things on the phone when we talk:

How's school?

How's basketball?

Maybe he'd ask more, but he's always interrupted by Michelle.*

*more on her later

As you've probably guessed, my parents are divorced. Which is no big deal, I know. So are every other kid's. But my mom works a lot, and even though she's a good parent and involved and all that, she's pretty tired out by the end of the day.

And since she had to work most of break and only wanted a few low-key Scrabble nights, that just added to the boredom.

I just got back to school. Guessing I'll be the only one happy to be here.

Definitely will be happy to be around my friends.

And pumped for my favorite classes, like PE and Ms. Laurie's art class. I started taking art this year, and I'm hooked. After our winter Zentangle project, I went home and made, like, five more Zentangle* drawings.

*a form of meditative doodling using structured patterns

ZEN-tastic

I'm at my locker before homeroom. Anthony, in full winter gear, walks over. That's what I love about the guy—he never cares what anyone thinks.

hat with side flaps

mittens

scarf

"deep freeze" parka

snow pants

snow boots

(probably keeps a bunch of quilts in locker)

Fortnite tonight?

You're on. Your house this time?

Yep.

Technically, we can play apart and talk on our phones, but it's way more fun in person. I love playing at his house, mainly 'cause of my gaming partner:

Anthony unloads about forty pounds of outerwear in his locker while I dump my slushy coat and hat in mine and grab my binder.

Anthony and I make our way through the jungle—aka main hall—trying to dodge a couple of scary-looking eighth graders (fourteen-year-olds with beards just isn't right).

Before winter break, Emmie Douglass wrote me a really mushy love letter that I wasn't supposed to see. Joe found it and showed it to me (and half the school). I guess he thought it was funny, but it was totally uncool of him to do that.

Even though she said she wrote it as a joke, I felt really bad that she was embarrassed. So I started talking to her. And didn't mention the note again. Now we're kinda friends and hang out in art.

We all crack up. I pretend to vomit, and that's the exact moment Celia walks by with her girl posse.

Now it's my turn to go Flamin' Cheetos. Celia is the queen bee of our class. We dated for two weeks in the beginning of seventh grade. Two of the longest weeks of my life.

After that, I gave up on dating in middle school. Which, by the way, is just holding hands in the hallway and surrendering half your french fries.

The three of us head to our homerooms—Anthony and I in one direction, Joe in another.

We walk in and see some guys from basketball. The season started last month, but we didn't have games or practice over break. We're so ready to get back to it, and we talk about our upcoming big game with Valley Bottom Middle. We've gotta beat them so we can go to the playoffs.

Mr. Fazekas blows in, red-faced from the cold, and takes roll.

I sneak-text Joe a meme of an evil-looking chipmunk in a popcorn bowl and label it:

Joe sends me:

I've missed these stupid sneaky school texts. I put my phone away and breathe in that familiar combo of textbooks, floor cleaner, and body spray.

I'm not worried about getting sick, and I'm excited about getting back into practice and stuff. But for some reason, Ethan's words give me a funny feeling.

The bell rings.

It's not even first period, and Ethan is already putting on the pressure?

He's worse than Coach Durdle.

All I wanna do is play.

Yeah, he's intense. But I get it. I wanna crush 'em, too.

Let's start by beating Ethan at practice. Maybe that'll shut him up.

We laugh and walk into science. Yeah, it feels good to be back.

Emmie

WE WALK TO HOMEROOM, WHERE I DAYDREAM SOME MORE ABOUT TYLER.

HE AND I HAVE BECOME SORT-OF FRIENDS. IT STARTED LAST MONTH WHEN BRI AND I WERE GOOFING OFF AT LUNCH.

27

TYLER

The day's going fast. I think it's because I'm not practicing my trumpet—or drawing it—to pass time during a blizzard.

Wall o' Winter Break Art

Plus our teachers are just getting back into the routine, so they've mostly just talked about their breaks and haven't piled on the schoolwork . . . yet.

vacay slides →

waiting for avalanche of assignments

Just getting to last period (aka the best one).

ART

At first, I feel like I'm walking into the wrong room. Instead of the desks put together to form a big square like they were before break, they're in regular rows.

Ms. Laurie sips smelly ginger tea in her usual mug:

She motions for us to sit anywhere. I pick a desk near the sink. Emmie walks in and—kinda cautiously—sits next to me.

We wait for the rest of the class to show up. Art is in the basement, so it can take a while to get here. Ms. Laurie knows this and usually doesn't give tardy slips if someone is a little late.

She reaches in her pocket and pulls out a phone.

She scrolls through her phone gallery. I can't help it, I admire the phone. Mine is really old (well, not **flip-phone** old like Emmie's

last one) and I cracked the glass. The upper-right corner looks
like a spiderweb and splits everything in twenty pieces.

She shows me a bunch of new sketches. Mainly hand studies,
but there's a really good contour drawing (we did those in the fall)
of her friend Brianna. And a colored-pencil still life of . . . I
can't make it out.

What are those?

Oh. Um, my mom eats really healthy food. That's a pack of multi-seed crackers, goji berries, some kale chips, and... a kiwi. I think.

I fished it out of the bottom drawer of my fridge.

I stare at the picture, including the black dented kiwi. Then I
look up at Emmie.

Ms. Laurie begins class by clearing her throat. She does this a lot. Probably why she needs the ginger tea.

Welcome back, everyone. Hope you all had good breaks.

Mr. Bob and I escaped to Charleston, South Carolina, to take some architectural photos.

Ms. Laurie is the only adult in the building with a preschool teacher's name. She hates being formal (also, her last name is Squalwinskarski; enough said). Mr. Bob is her husband. They're both photographers. "Professional hobby," she calls it. Mr. Bob is a podiatrist or taxidermist or something by day.

Well, time to get back in the swing of things, right?

We're going to kick January off with a really fun project. At least, _I_ think it'll be fun.

She holds up a bunch of graphic novels, comic books, and manga magazines that are sitting on her desk.

MANGA madness

COMIX

Any of you into comics?

Comics are a great way to tell a story _and_ express yourself artistically.

And that's what you're going to do for the next three weeks. I'd like you guys to create your own comic.

The room explodes with excitement.

There are some rules and non-rules. You can use any medium and material you'd like.

It must be eight to ten pages. And there's no assigned subject. The sky's the limit!

When they're finished, you'll be able to display your stories in the Student Showcase at the end of the month.

I'll award a prize for the best piece.

kids murmuring

This sounds seriously cool. First, we never get a chance to work on anything for that long. I always feel like I'm rushing to finish every project.

Second, a PRIZE! I live for competition.

The Student Showcase is an actual event. It's held on a Friday night, and parents are invited. We get to see students' stuff on display, like science and history dioramas, art projects, poetry, and short stories. Basically, it's a whole big "school spirit" thing—but instead of sports, it's for academics and arts.

As cool as this sounds, it suddenly hits me that I've never tried making my own comics.

You'd be good at an animal story or something. Since you like drawing them.

Yeah, maybe. I've never done a comic before. I mean, I've read 'em, and I've drawn cartoony things, I guess. But I've never made up a whole story.

That's the part that kinda scares me.

ha ha

Emmie gets quiet for a moment.

What if we did one together?

You mean team up?

Yeah. We can write the story together. Help each other. Maybe illustrate our own chapters and combine them or something.

I think. I'd hate to drag her down in case I'm bad at this. But then again, how bad can I be? Emmie's a better artist, but I'm still pretty good. Plus it would be fun to brainstorm and bounce ideas off each other. That's the stuff I like to do. Teamwork.

Okay, let's try!

We walk over to Ms. Laurie's desk. There are a gajillion art pens, markers, and knickknacks on it.

Ms. Laurie?

44

She looks up.

She thinks for a bit, concentrating on a elephant figurine wearing an artist's smock.

Okay, then. You're a team!

I high-five Emmie. She just misses my hand.

oops

I laugh and we head back to our desks.

I hope I did the right thing by partnering up. I don't always think stuff through.

impulsive

(was once a 22-point Scrabble word)

Her excitement is contagious.

Yeah, this can work.

In fact . . .

... this'll be fun!

Emmie

OMG. I'M PARTNERED WITH TYLER. OMG.

I WISH BRI WERE HERE SO I COULD SCREAM WITH HER.

I TURN TO A NEW PAGE IN MY SKETCHBOOK. MY FAVORITE THING IS SEEING A FRESH WHITE SHEET OF PAPER, ALL READY TO BE COVERED IN DRAWINGS AND IDEAS.

SUDDENLY, I HAVE AN IDEA. SOMETHING THAT I THINK WE'D BOTH LIKE.

I SKETCH FOR A BIT, 'CAUSE I THINK IT'D BE MORE EXCITING TO HAVE AN ACTUAL IMAGE TO GO WITH THE IDEA.

TYLER

Lunch.

It's the day after the comics project announcement. I sit with Anthony, Joe, and a few other seventh graders from the basketball team. The volleyball girls sit near us.

Second Lunch Period (a handy blueprint):

We're pretty close to the entrance, which lets us see who's walking in. In Celia's case, this is very important.

My older brother, Zach, used to sit at my table. He's kind of a legend.

You'd think I'd have trouble filling his shoes, but being friendly and good at sports help. Or maybe the whole popularity thing is genetic.

parents

Or not.

Today is Pasta Day. That's just a fancy way of saying "spaghetti with red sauce and meatbombs."

mushy pasta

runny sauce

granite block

Luckily, I brought my lunch. Joe is eating spaghetti and talking while meatbomb shrapnel flies out of his mouth.

I spot Emmie and Brianna walking to their usual table.

Great.

I turn back to my lunch, which I'm no longer hungry for.

Usually I've got the appetite of someone three times my size.

The other guys laugh.

Now I'm irritated **and** not hungry. I resort to a solid redirection strategy. I take a huge bite out of my PB and banana sandwich and open my mouth to show Joe. That starts a "see-food" war at the table.

It worked. Once the lunch monitor threatens us with detention, we settle down.

My voice trails off.

He makes kissing noises as I clamp my hand over his mouth.

Oh crud, what if Emmie hears or worse . . . ?

Whew.

Quickly, I check to see if Emmie and Brianna were listening. Luckily, they're far enough away, and the cafeteria is really loud. Not to mention:

Not sure why I care, anyway. Celia always shoots her mouth off. And as for Joe, he cracks jokes—that's his thing. No big deal.

My appetite returns, and I scarf down my lunch while we talk about the Valley Bottom game.

> Remember? Last time I barely had a stupid cold, and she put Ryan Keiser in. He can't even dribble.

> I could be *dead* and I'd still run circles around him.

Not starting is the worst. I'd rather grow a third arm and burst into blue zits than not be in the starting lineup. I couldn't face my friends.

> It'd be stupid not to put you in.

> Well, you can bet I'm not gonna miss any practice. No way am I gonna chance it.

I'm starting to feel weird about meeting with Emmie. Maybe Ethan's right. I shouldn't chance it, even if it's just for half an hour. The comics project is cool, but this game is way more important, and it's in two weeks.

The bell rings.

She takes out her sketchbook (which she always has on her).

I get a lump in my throat. Emmie's sketches are really good, and she's already farther along than me. There won't be enough time to draw **and** start writing our comic story in art.

Also, I just wanna work on this. Her drawings are totally motivating. We can win the art prize!

You know what? Never mind, I'll be there.

Really?

Yeah. I won't miss that much practice. It's fine.

She looks so happy.

We separate just as Joe and Anthony come up.

We head out at the same time as Celia and her posse. Once again, she looks at me and then at Emmie. And grins wickedly.

She gives us an epic eye roll and heads off with her giggling band of followers.

The second bell rings, which gets us moving. Joe and I are gonna be late for band. We both play trumpet (badly).

And I mean it.

Up in the ATTIC

by Emmie Douglass & Tyler Ross

THE BOY lives in a typical house. With typical parents. He does typical things.

house →
parents ↓↓
regular tree ↘

He hangs out with his friends.

The Boy ↓
freckle →
Adam ↙
Jon ↘

What's in a ghost's nose?

BOOgers. Har.

↑ stupid joke

He goes to school.

Swampfront Middle School ↙

another tree ↘

He reads comics.

Cap'n Underthings ↓

(Hoppin') MAD magazine ↗

BUT...

He also paints awesome skateboards.

manga

skull

hipster dude

waves

He has an attic hangout with a blanket fort.

bed-sheets

old stuff

flashlight

comics

In it, he reads, paints, and draws his own comics. All in private.

None of his friends know.

That's because he likes having his own space and thoughts away from school and stuff.

And that's why, underneath, **THE BOY** isn't so typical after all.

(cont'd...)

Emmie

WE'RE MAKING TWO MAIN
CHARACTERS FOR OUR STORY:
ONE FOR ME, ONE FOR HIM.
THEY'LL HAVE THEIR OWN
CHAPTERS AND SWITCH OFF.

BUT FIRST, WE'RE GONNA WRITE
THE ENTIRE STORY TOGETHER.
THAT'S WHAT WE'RE DOING
TODAY.

THE GIRL is always alone.

She used to have friends.

Back when she was alive.

RIP

That was a long time ago. Now she wanders by herself, unless she happens upon a passing spirit.

She loves exploring homes. That's where she watches humans live their lives.

bark

She really loves attics.

Attics: where precious memories are stored.

The Retro Years

old photos

old clothes

old furniture

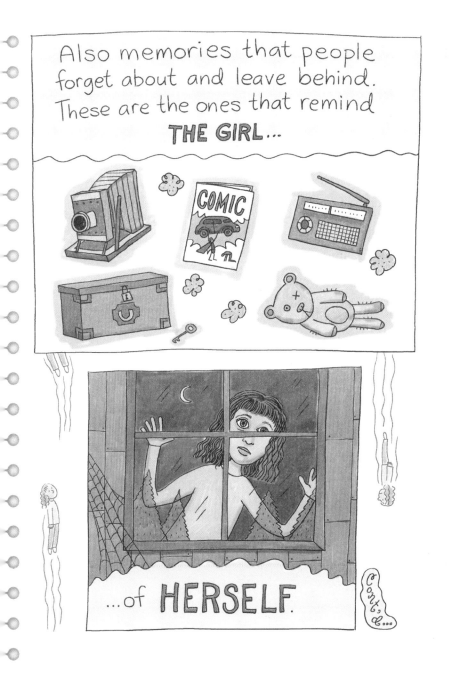

Also memories that people forget about and leave behind. These are the ones that remind

THE GIRL...

...of **HERSELF.**

Cont,d...

TYLER

I'm sitting on my bed, sketching out a comics page (and avoiding all my other homework), when my phone goes off.

I can set my clock by this conversation. There's nothing more predictable.

Still, I'm glad he called. He's pretty good about calling a lot, like a couple times a week. That's 'cause I don't get to see him much. Only during Thanksgiving and spring break. He lives far away, in Seattle. We used to visit during summers, but as we got older, Zach and I wanted to stay closer to home for sports camp and friends and stuff.

It's not like he has a lot of time for visits, anyway. My dad's a big-shot lawyer. He has a swanky condo downtown that he shares with his girlfriend, Michelle (another lawyer). She's okay, but it's obvious she's not that crazy about kids. Also, their place is really modern and not family friendly. The only decorations are some bizarre abstract paintings and expensive-looking, geometrical knickknacks. Crystal orbs and cubes.

yelled at me for holding orb

almost made me drop it, ironically

Dad doesn't visit us much, either. He grew up in Seattle, and he barely has any ties left here. Just a few work friends and us.

The one thing he will do when we visit him is shoot hoops. He used to coach rec league—that's how Zach and I got hooked. Too bad Seattle isn't always the best place to play b-ball outside.

150 average days of rain

(cool Space Needle)

Make sure you watch your follow-through. And the rebound.

I know....

We talk a little more about the game, but I'm starting to get impatient. Which is a first. Usually I can talk hoops forever.

But I really wanna get back to drawing.

I'm about to make up an excuse when I hear Michelle in the background.

mumble mumble

Hey, buddy, gotta go. Catch you on the weekend?

Sure.

Big surprise. I can't remember the last time Michelle didn't interrupt us. You'd think knowing how little my dad sees us, she'd be okay with our FaceTiming. I swear she butts into everything. Zach and I used to joke that she'd interrupt our weddings.

I shake it off. It could be worse. Michelle's not my favorite person, but (as my mom reminds us) she's no evil Disney stepmother.

Michelle and Disney stepmothers: a comparison		
	MICHELLE	EVIL STEPMOM
cruel	✗	✓
wicked	✗	✓
dislikes kids	(ish)	✓
feeds kids poisoned apples	✗	✓
interrupts FaceTime	✓	✗

After I hang up, I reach for my sketchbook. That's when a huge rumbling almost makes me drop it. It's not an earthquake, though.

rrrumble

Time for my hundredth snack of the day. I head downstairs and make a beeline for the pantry. My mom is at the table, typing at her laptop and wearing her noise-canceling headphones.

I stop to take a breath. Ever since I turned thirteen, it feels like I can't get enough to eat. Like I need twenty bags of chips for every growing bone in my body.

food math:

$$CHIPS \times 20 = femur$$

94

Somehow, my mom has a knack for translating snack-speak.

She jokes, but mismatched socks wouldn't be a surprise. My mom's a financial consultant. Outwardly, she's not very put-together (think: skirts and sneaks), but inwardly, she's really organized. She has to be. Even though she's busy and tired, she runs this house practically by herself.

She's not wrong. As a little kid, all I did was draw. Just like Emmie. Getting back into it now, it feels like I never stopped.

Mom gives me a little Queen of England wave while I head upstairs. I can't help noticing she is wearing two different socks.

bass
guitar
wailing

chip crumbs

I consider knocking on Zach's door to say hi, but he'd probably throw his jar of picks at me. Zach doesn't like to be bothered when he's playing.

I take my sketchpad and plop on the bed. An eraser and some stray Skittles fly off. If my mom knew I had snacks up here, she'd kill me.

I go back to sketching. I already have two-and-a-half pages done, which is something. I don't think I've ever been this hooked on a school project.

Too bad it's already caused me to be late to practice twice: once that first day after school with Emmie, and then again yesterday when I realized I left my sketchbook in the art room and needed (okay, wanted) to bring it home. I ended up thinking of a great idea right then and had to get it down before I forgot. Totally lost track of time.

gulp

Anyway, I promised myself I wouldn't be late again. Ever. Especially if I wanna beat Valley Bottom. **And** make point guard in high school like a certain someone.

Besides . . .

. . . it's not like this art project is gonna last forever.

STILL, I WONDER HOW CONFIDENT KIDS DO IT. KIDS WHO — EVEN IF THEY DO SAY DUMB STUFF — NEVER SEEM TO WORRY ABOUT IT.

LIKE HIM

Whoa. Nice kilt, lassie.

Thanks.

He's being sarcastic.

I know. But I like to pretend he isn't. It helps.

SUDDENLY,
MY STOMACH GETS THAT
BAD SQUEEZY FEELING.

Freak.

IF THEY SAY THESE THINGS
ABOUT SARAH...

...DO THEY ALSO SAY STUFF
ABOUT <u>ME</u>?

TYLER

Basketball practice. I'm trying not to miss as much. I did skip a couple days ago when Emmie and I had to brainstorm some stuff for the last pages (told Coach I had an orthodontist appointment. Yeah, I know, not proud). Luckily, we got a lot done in class today. We're almost halfway through. And we would've done more if we hadn't kept getting sidetracked.

The more we worked, the more we talked, and the more annoyed

Ms. Laurie got.

I don't have to guess who they're talking about.

Zach

I shoot again. This time I make it.

Everyone on our team worships Zach. Especially the eighth graders who remember him when they were sixth-grade peons waiting to get off the bench.

Truth is, I'm almost as good. Zach used to play pickup with me at home and taught me a lot of techniques.

I can tell Anthony and the other guys are a little miffed at me. They don't think I'm taking the game seriously enough, which is flat-out untrue.

It's not that I'm not committed, it's just . . .

. . . maybe I'm not as . . .

. . . obsessed about it?

Malik passes me the ball and I (barely) score.

Anthony high-fives me but not enthusiastically. He doesn't get peeved often. He's easygoing, like me, and keeps a lot of stuff inside (also like me).

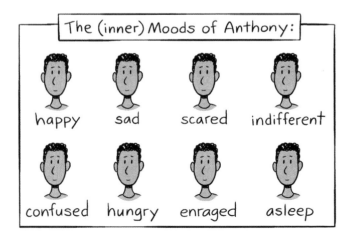

The (inner) Moods of Anthony:

happy   sad   scared   indifferent

confused   hungry   enraged   asleep

We've both been into basketball ever since I can remember. That's what unites us.

Also, we've always gone to each other's homes after school for pickup. Once we hit sixth grade, we added Joe to our mix, although he's terrible. But he's a great supporter. He comes to all our games and cracks jokes to cheer us up if we play lousy.

When we played at my house, Zach (before he got busy) used to join us and teach us stuff, including his famous hook shot. That one's still hit or miss, but I'm determined to perfect it by high school.

Everyone. If we don't improve, we won't beat Valley Bottom. If we don't beat Valley Bottom, we won't go to the playoffs.

And if we don't go to the playoffs, I won't get Coach of the Year for the third time in a row. This is important!

We fall back into scrimmage.

Told you you're zoning.

Maybe it's that artsy girl he hangs with. It's always a girl.

We're just friends.

That's what we thought about Cee until you two started wearing matching outfits.

They all laugh. I start to get mad. Why do I feel like the butt
of everyone's jokes? Good thing Joe isn't here.

And how do I convince them that I **do** take the game seriously
and that I'm **not** distracted by a girl?

My anger fuels me. I grab the ball from Anthony's hands,
run to the three-point-line, and . . .

Anthony gives me a half smile.

But he doesn't look convinced.

One night in the attic, THE BOY reads a ghost story.

spooky comic

He never believed in ghosts, but for the first time...

I wonder if they exist!

flashlight face

The story talks about ghost hunting.

TOOLS:

EMF detector

camera (the good kind)

digital recorder ↓ (or phone app)

thermal scanner

Emmie

I'M IN THE LIBRARY FOR STUDY HALL, DRAWING AND PEOPLE-WATCHING.

ABOUT 2% OF THE KIDS ARE ACTUALLY STUDYING. THE OTHER 98% ARE GOOFING OFF WHILE TRYING TO STAY UNDER THE RADAR.

IT'S FRIDAY. BRI AND I USUALLY TAKE TURNS SLEEPING AT EACH OTHER'S HOUSES. IT USED TO BE AT MY HOUSE UNTIL BRI'S DAD FINISHED HIS BASEMENT. WE SET UP AN OLD TENT, DECORATED IT, AND NOW...

...WE GLAMP!

SARAH JOINED US ONCE BEFORE BREAK. BRI WASN'T THRILLED, BUT SHE PRETENDED TO BE.

So fun.

SHE DOESN'T LIKE SARAH MUCH. I USED TO THINK IT WAS BECAUSE EVEN COMPARED TO US, SARAH'S A LITTLE ON THE... DIFFERENT SIDE.

BUT NOW I'M PRETTY SURE IT'S 'CAUSE SHE THINKS SARAH IS A THIRD WHEEL. I KEEP HOPING BRI WILL COME AROUND.

MY CHEEKS GET HOT. WHY DOES EVERYONE PICK ON HER? BECAUSE SHE'S DIFFERENT?

MAYBE... *TOO* DIFFERENT?

BRI SNAPS ME OUT OF MY THOUGHTS.

What's Joe got against her?

THAT'S A FIRST.

Signs of the Apocalypse:

Locusts descending

Heavens raining fire

Bri sticking up for Sarah

SHE LEAVES AND I START DRAWING AGAIN.

scritch scritch scritch

SOMETIMES I WORRY THAT TYLER WILL COME TO HIS SENSES AND STOP BEING FRIENDS WITH ME.

It's not like I fit in with him, Joe, and the rest of that crowd.

In fact, I only have two other friends and they're not exactly cool, either.

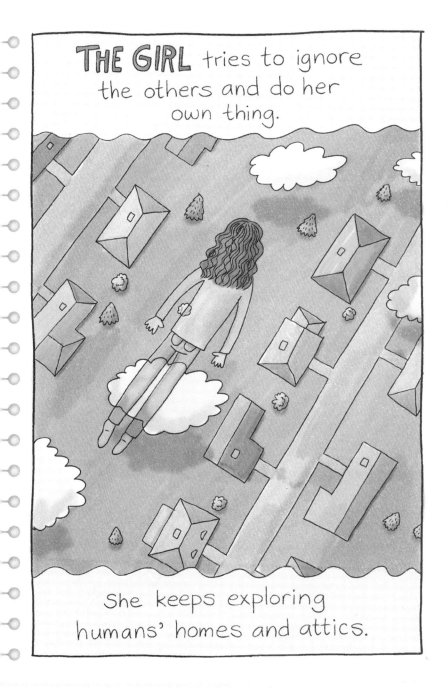

THE GIRL tries to ignore the others and do her own thing.

She keeps exploring humans' homes and attics.

Cont'd...

TYLER

I come home to a familiar sound.

thunka
thunka
thunka

It's, like, unusually warm out. Almost fifty degrees. I only know that 'cause our science teacher, Mr. Danker, gives us updates every twenty minutes.

Northeast winds 5-10 mph...

lost dream of becoming a meteorologist

Even though it's the second week of January, all the snow has melted and the sun's out. That's one way to be fooled into thinking it's spring.

The other:

Guys in shorts

pale legs
skinny legs
overly hairy legs

No practice today, so I stayed at school a little late to work on the comic book. Emmie had a dentist appointment, so it was just me, Emo Girl, and two kids from Manga Club.

sticking out like a

On my way out, I almost bumped into Celia, who just had volleyball practice.

I didn't say anything. I was too mad. I just shoved past her and knew the perfect comeback would probably hit me in the middle of the night.

Stuff like this has been going on ever since Emmie and I teamed up for the comic book. It's making me really . . . well . . .

Zach and his two best friends, Jonathan and Eli, are playing pickup in our driveway. I wish I could join them to blow off some steam, but I have homework to do. Also, they probably don't want a seventh grader invading their turf. They're cool guys, though. Eli reminds me of Anthony, super chill. Jonathan is all high energy. He's a small forward at Lakefront High. Eli is a shooting guard, and Zach, of course, is a point guard . . . an unofficial leader. Even as a sophomore, he earned it.

That's my goal for high school, too. Malik is our point guard now but not for long.

Also, I promised myself to step it up. After today, I'm gonna give it my all at practice, get back to the Y this weekend, and beat Valley Bottom!

The guys take a break as I approach.

He's just joking about the nickname, but I cringe, anyway. Being popular in middle school means nothing to high schoolers. I'll always just be the little baby brother.

Jonathan wipes his forehead with the hem of his T-shirt, and Zach chugs Gatorade, which my mom calls "sugar soup."

I'm a little testy when I say that. Zach knows my b-ball goals.

It would be nice if he actually **helped** me with 'em.

Maybe Jonathan's thinking the same thing.

I have so much homework, and I should do it now so I can finally play Fortnite with Anthony later, but I can't resist. Playing with (good) high schoolers is next-level awesome.

I team up with Zach—who's the best player—so it's even.

We play for about fifteen minutes when . . .

YOW!

Zach runs inside to get some ice while I sit on the cement and think the worst.

Zach comes back with the ice and I keep it on my ankle. The guys give me a pep talk, saying they've done the same kind of stuff, but I'm miserable. I can't believe I hurt myself!

I tell Mom what happened, and she and Zach walk me inside. I sit on the couch, depressed.

It should be okay, honey. Looks pretty minor. Ice, elevate, and you'll be okay for the game.

between Zach and me, has seen enough sports injuries to know

But I would skip practice for a day or two.

I groan. Coach will not be happy.

Want me to stay?

Nah, it's okay. I've gotta do homework, anyway.

He musses my hair and heads back out. He's being extra nice. Maybe I should injure myself more often.

My mom hovers for a while, concerned. But my ankle is starting to feel better.

It's okay, you can go. I'm fine.

You sure, honey? I can make you something. I was thinking about some comfort food tonight. Lasagna?

The only thing scarier than my mom making boxed or bagged dinners is her attempt to make meals from scratch.

flashback to the green soup incident

was supposed to be chicken noodle

"here you go, Ty

Zach and I got used to making our own meals whenever she worked late. Zach makes the world's best panini, and I nailed Spaghetti à la Ty.

cheese sauce with red pepper flakes

The window faces the front yard. I hear Zach and his friends playing again.

thunka thunka

They're sophomores and don't go to prom or anything, but they have dances and stuff. Zach, Eli, and Jonathan were all part of the "Sweet Six," which is the tenth-grade version of a homecoming court. Six guys and six girls. The name is gag-worthy, but it's a such huge deal that the guys don't mind.

(...or they put up with it)

cringing

Sweet six
Sweet six
Sweet six

Reminds me of what I could be. Me and my friends. All of us, with our dorky crowns, waving from the stage.

paired with Celia

shudder

Sometimes it's hard being related to Zach. It feels like there's a lot to live up to. Especially when your older brother is . . . well . . .

Reigning prince of Lakefront High (to be king in two years)

Bow, peons.

My phone goes off.

Hey, loser! My mom's taking me to Taystee's. Wanna come?

Can't. Homework.

I don't tell Joe about my ankle. For some reason, I don't want it to get back to Anthony.

Actually, Joe's a lot shorter than me. He used to get picked on for being so little. But back in elementary school, he started deflecting with jokes. You know, making fun of himself before anyone else could.

Then he started deflecting by making fun of others.

Not the most mature thing to do, but it was one way to get kids to stop picking on him. He also got a reputation for being a clown, which won him some friends, like us. And predictably, some enemies.

Joe can be kinda polarizing, but if there's one thing he is, it's loyal. Proven by an incident at the beginning of sixth grade.

There was this mangy cat that used to roam around the field behind our school. She liked to hunt and leave behind dead rodents and birds.

dead pigeon →

could smell it from the science room →

One day, Joe, Anthony, and I decided it would be funny if we left one of her "presents" at our most hated teacher's desk: Mr. Dromacelli. He was awful—gave us mean nicknames (mine was "Fang" for my snaggletooth before braces), and made us **stand up** if he called on us in class.

uh...er...

imaginary spotlight on fang

Anyway, he was not amused by the rotting chipmunk we left in a shoebox on his desk chair—which he almost sat on. He was sure it was us 'cause, well, we weren't exactly angels. First, he made Joe go to the principal. Anthony and I knew we were next.

But Joe took the heat.

Nah, it was just me. The others would never think of anything so hilarious.

Anthony and I were so impressed (and relieved!), we made up for it by bringing Joe treats for detention. He especially loved my mom's rainbow Jell-O squares.

detention essay on rodents

rainbow stain

So that's why we hang out with Joe despite his big mouth. He'd stick with us through thick, thin . . . and dead rodents.

At that, my temper flares.

Sometimes I think Joe gets away with everything. Even after the rodent thing, he joked his way out of an extra week of detention.

I am, but not at him.

I hang up and fume.

It's one thing for Anthony to get in my face, but now he's saying things behind my back? I grab my phone again.

I put my phone down. I'm so mad, I can't even do homework.

Instead, I reach into my backpack and pull out my sketchbook. I pick up where I left off in my story. I don't even glance at the outline or anything. I have most of it memorized, anyway.

I draw and draw until I lose track of time. I even forget about my ankle.

And I realize . . .

. . . this is the only thing that makes me feel better.

Emmie

RESTROOM BREAK.

giggle

She is so extra.

me

citrus body spray (smells like cheese)

I know. Last time there was some kind of snake on her chest.

I think it was s'posed to be a flower stem, but still. Look, I took a picture of it.

GRACE THROWS ME A
WEIRD LOOK. GUILT
MAYBE.

Or pity.

THEY LEAVE IN A HURRY.
I HEAR THEM OUTSIDE
THE DOOR.

(giggle) Busted.

By Tyler's downgrade.

MY STOMACH DROPS.

Downgrade?

PLOP

163

TYLER

It's been three days since I twisted my ankle. My mom was right: it feels fine now. I was lucky. But I had to miss practice the last two days. Coach wasn't pleased, but she understood.

always excuses sports injuries

I'm in art class. Emmie's acting kinda weird. She's hiding her face and is super quiet, even for her. Then again, I've been pretty quiet, too.

two muffled mice

Silence again while we get back to the book. We're each working a little differently. Emmie's sketching all her pages first, then inking them, then adding color. I'm doing all the sketching, inking, and coloring as I go. We're both doing a pretty good job of sticking to the "script," although sometimes we'll ask each other if we can make small changes here and there. It's a good system.

It reminds me of basketball. You have to work as a team; otherwise it falls apart. Strategies are mapped out, and if we follow 'em, it usually goes our way. If we deviate, it can go either way.

Today I'm deviating. I'm kinda rushing this page.

also *looks* like I'm rushing

I feel bad. It's not Emmie's fault I injured myself and got behind.

After laying off my ankle, I had to get back at it. The weather stayed warm-ish, and I was able to play in the driveway yesterday. Luckily, I was sinking more balls than missing. Zach even joined me once.

giving tips

semi-listening

It didn't last long, though.

I look down at my paper.

rushed drawings

looks like a first grader took over

I growl, crumple the page, and toss it in the trash.

Ms. Laurie comes over.

How's it going, Tyler?

I messed up.

Anything I can help you with?

Ms. Laurie has been checking our work as we go.

I am, but I'm trying to keep up with Emmie. I know I should slow down. I work a lot better when I do. Some kids are fast and good. I'm slow and good. And I like lots of detail.

And I really, really like working on this. I guess I'm just upset about missing practice. I wanna win the game, **and** I want to win that art prize.

Without realizing I'm doing it, I put my head in my hands and:

I look up and find Emmie looking right back at me curiously.

But I'm not in the mood to be watched.

She immediately turns away, but I can see she's getting red

and tears are forming.

Argh! I hate it when girls cry.

I think for a moment.

You wanna come over Saturday? We can work on it then.

Her eyes get really wide—happy wide—like I just offered her Phineas.

SLORP!

giggle

licked entire face off

T-to your house?

Sure. I'm practicing in the morning, but maybe after.

Um. Okay.

I hold up my palm and she high-fives it.

Good. Doing this at my house means getting more done. In private. Away from other people. People who make comments.

Yeah, privacy is what we need.

The thought of it makes me feel better already.

Emmie

WOOSH

AN HOUR LATER, WE'RE IN MY ROOM.

I DIDN'T TELL BRI ABOUT THE GIRLS IN THE BATHROOM. BUT SHE'S RIGHT. I'VE BEEN AVOIDING SARAH EVER SINCE.

YESTERDAY:

Hi. I had a makeup test and took the later lunch. Can I eat with you guys?

THIS IS WHERE MY PLAN
COMES IN. IF I WANNA
BE COOL ENOUGH FOR
TYLER *AND* EARN HIS
FRIENDS' RESPECT, I'VE
GOTTA DO TWO THINGS:

It looks like he's searching for something.

Could it be?

REC

THE GIRL had never seen a human <u>look</u> for those like her. Usually they were too scared.

Wow.

This is new.

Or didn't believe.

TYLER

Having the usual post-dinner FaceTime call with my dad.

full of frozen
fajitas

You ready for the game?

Sure.

How's your bank shot? Improving?

Uh-huh.

He's trying to keep it light, but I'm not in the mood.

Why am I bothering? All he cares about are sports and grades. He never says anything about art, and he knows I'm into that, too.

Michelle pokes her head into the screen. Right where the cracks are.

multiple Michelles →

Hi, Ty! Sorry to bother, but I need your dad! Somebody's gotta walk Petey* and I have to cook!

*a cat. They walk a cat.

Michelle is one of those people who speaks entirely in exclamation points. Doesn't matter if she's happy, angry, or confused.

Okay, gotta go. Bye, son.

Click. Record time. Six minutes until she nabbed him.

Barely a second later, I get another FaceTime call.

Dude! Come over. Fortnite marathon.

Joe needs you to watch me KICK BOTH YOUR BUTTS.

(About the Anthony thing: I'm trying to let it go)

I laugh and am about to hang up when:

196

I don't tell them she's coming over Saturday.

With that, Phineas sticks his face in front of the camera and licks it, his giant tongue taking up the screen.

They hang up, and I flop on my back and stare at my ceiling. Definitely not in the mood to study now.

So my friends think I'm blowing them off. And losing my edge. I'm not!

Am I?

eyeing my sketchbook comics

And they think Emmie's my girlfriend! Come on.

Can't I be friends with a girl? What's wrong with that? Anthony is tight with Jaime.

YAP
YAP
YAP

(everyone just stopped thinking they were a couple)

'Course, they've been friends forever. Emmie's only been my friend for a couple months. Also, she's not . . . well . . . like Jaime or the others.

Sometimes I wish that Emmie wasn't so . . . different or some-thing. Quiet. Artsy. Then maybe people wouldn't make such a big deal of us hanging out.

I know it's not her fault. But I can't help feeling . . .

Enough. I sit up. Gonna forget all this and get a snack. I heave myself off the bed, making more secret Skittles fly off.

I almost bump into Zach coming out of his room.

I groan. Not that again.

Zach shrugs and starts heading downstairs.

Hey...Z.

He looks up.

Does Dad ever talk to you about anything other than... I dunno, basketball?

(ha) Rarely. Unless it's about college. Or if I have a girlfriend. There's no way I'll tell him about Arianna. I don't need the third degree.

I nod.

I change my mind about the snack.

Miracles:

Noses parts the sea

Statues weep

I'm no longer hungry

flop

Here's one more miracle:

Emmie

I GO TO MY LOCKER TO GRAB MY (COMFIER) GYM SHOES.

FOR A SECOND, I FEEL SOMETHING ALMOST LIKE...BETRAYAL.

BRI'S NOT S'POSED TO TALK TO HER. OR EVEN <u>LIKE</u> HER.

Why now, when I want her out of my life?

I PUT ON MY GYM SHOES AND HEAD TO (UGH) PE...

snap

still doing jig

TYLER

History class.

Everyone laughs. First time Mr. Musko ever broke out of his monotone.

The bell rings.

218

Soon they get enough dirty looks (and one hall monitor's glare) to straighten up and attempt to walk like regular human beings.

... or seventh graders (slouchy)

How's your bank shot? Been practicing?

You sound like my dad.

What do you want me to sound like? Tonight's the game.

I try to stay ... What's that word? That word Emmie says her mom uses a lot.

Yeah, been trying to hold my zen for a while now.

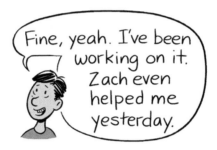

Fine, yeah. I've been working on it. Zach even helped me yesterday.

That's a lie.

It's a sign of the Apocalypse.

That makes me laugh, in a depressing way.

Truth is, I'm kinda nervous for tonight. And Anthony harping about the game isn't helping. Normally when I'm nervous for a game, it's a good kind of nervous.

But today, it feels like there are worms crawling around in my gut.

Ms. Laurie appears in the hall, on her way to the teachers' lounge.

mystery room

secret gaming room?

throwback sixties lounge?

Fourth Dimension?

It's always weird seeing teachers out of their rooms. Even weirder to see them in the wild.

also plain wrong

slorp

(Mr. Musko)

Joe and Anthony snicker at her preschool name. I shove them.

Joe and Anthony snort.

I shove him again.

And, of course, right at that moment:

Joe and Anthony burst into laughter. Emmie gets all red and looks confused. She ducks into math so fast, you'd think she actually liked the class.

Coach Durdle walks by. She sees me and stops.

And hesitates.

I have a couple minutes before class starts. The guys give me a questioning look and walk into the room. Coach and I stand in the hallway a little farther from the door. I feel a weird sense of dread.

Tyler... I don't know how to say this...

I'm afraid you're going to have to sit out tonight.

At first, this doesn't register.

Then it hits.

WHAT??

Hopefully? No, no, no. I have to play! I can't miss the most important game before playoffs!

She doesn't say anything. But I can see she's thinking it over.

I give her the saddest, most pleading look that I save for my mom whenever I mess up at home.

Coach fires back her sternest look.

But then her eyes get all soft.

I walk into class and sit down, feeling like my brain ran a marathon.

I can't tell him. I just can't.

Mrs. Dietrich arrives at that moment. We get started.

My wormy gut lurches. This day is turning into a roller coaster.

THE BOY lies in his fort and looks through his photos.

He finds...

... nothing.

Discouraged, he deletes the pictures and tosses his spooky comic book aside.

Emmie

I LAUGH. TRUTH IS, I'M PARTLY GOING TO SEE TYLER PLAY...

AND PARTLY 'CAUSE THIS IS WHAT THE COOLER KIDS DO... GO TO GAMES.

All part of The Plan to fit in.

I don't think I'm *dragging* you since Anthony plays, too.

Nuh-uh. I never wanted to sit in the stands with all their friends. Still don't.

But I will. Thanks, B. I *do* owe you.

You can buy me a greasy hot dog.

I LOOK DOWN AND INSPECT MYSELF.

cute-casual outfit

stylish hand-me-down sweater from sister

sporty purse I got with babysitting $$

favorite jeans with holes (on purpose)

FIRST BASKETBALL GAME. NEW ME.

Maybe Tyler will even notice me. As more than a friend.

242

(cont'd...)

TYLER

All eyes are on me.

But I'm not nervous anymore. And even though I just missed the last free throw, I'm super focused. I can make this one.

Ready.

Aim.

Shoot.

grooan

I hear the groans and boos. Malik gives me a reassuring pat on the back as we settle into our positions.

I'm so upset, I can't see straight. We're behind by two. Freaking. Points.

And it's not just those I missed. All night, my shooting's been erratic.

↰ "Winn Word"

I look at Coach Durdle. She nods grimly at me. She took a huge chance when she finally agreed to let me play.

I've gotta make it up to her.

Luckily, in the last quarter we catch up. Ethan and Anthony score six points. Valley Bottom also gets six. And finally . . .

YES!!

Ross the Boss is *baaack!*

Twenty seconds later, the buzzer sounds. We won. Barely.

Everyone's excited by the last-minute win. Coach Durdle even lets out a:

WHOOP!

So does my mom, who's sitting in the first row of bleachers.

WHOOOOP!

a duet

But I'm shook. If this all-over-the-place playing keeps up, I'm never gonna make point guard. I'll be lucky if Coach keeps starting me the rest of the season. If Zach were here, he'd be shaking his head. I'm glad he's not. He has late practice at the high school.

I try to look on the bright side. We **did** win. And I made the winning shot! At least it was exciting. And now we get to go to the playoffs!

251

We glare at each other, and I feel this close to popping him, but I see Coach Durdle eyeing us to go shake hands with the other team. So we separate, Anthony and I giving each other the stink eye.

I don't believe this. Anthony and I haven't argued since fifth grade when he copied my science worksheet, including all the wrong answers and one specific one where we had to name a star after us. We both got in trouble.

Name a star after you.

Red Dwarf Ross

How many planets

Name a star after you.

RED DWARF Ross

How many planets

I try to find my inner zen (again). We shake the other team's hands and head toward the locker room near the stands. That's when I see Emmie and Brianna, a few benches up. It's not hard to spot them; middle school games are always half full at best.

uh-oh.

Hey, Ty, your number one fan!

Or his girlfriend/ not-girlfriend.

S#@% shut up.

clamp

I know Tyler Ross would never say something like that because Tyler Ross knows better.

Great. On top of everything, I got in trouble. And third-personed.

Coach, I wasn't—

I stop. There's no way I'm gonna rat my friends out.

Sorry.

She nods and goes to talk to the other coach while we walk to the locker room. Some of the guys are smirking at me while checking out Emmie.

Who is looking at them and me, confused. Or embarrassed. Or both.

But I don't care. I'm so tired of all the teasing and trash talk. Even if it's just joking. It's no longer funny.

I don't wave back.

Emmie

BRI'S EYES LIGHT UP AS ANTHONY DRIBBLES THE BALL ACROSS THE COURT AND SCORES.

Em, what are we doing here? It's fun watching those two, but this isn't our thing.

And it's not even that crowded. Mostly families and a bunch of their friends.

GULP! WHAT SHOULD I DO? SMILE? WAVE?

I REALIZE MY HAND IS STILL IN THE AIR. I PUT IT DOWN.

TYLER

Just got home from the game. Usually I'd go to Taystee's for hot chocolate afterward (always after a win), but I wasn't in the mood. Instead, I'm curled up under my mom's favorite old Sherpa blanket, watching TV.

Comfort stuff:
✓ thick blanket
✓ squishy couch
✓ cheese curls
✓ cartoon rerun
✓ big fluffy dog
   (I wish!)

My phone goes off.

I open the app. I barely have to scroll to see that a dozen kids

posted the same meme.

old pic of
Celia and me

bad
cut-paste
job of
Emmie's
face

WHEN YOUR EX
HAS A GLOW-DOWN

I go cold.

I text that to Joe.

This isn't happening. This has to be Celia and her friends. No one else I know would do this.

I wait for about two years until Joe texts back. I use all my willpower not to open SnapGab.

Not sure if I believe that. I just hope Emmie didn't see it.

imaginary screaming

AHHHH

first time anyone would hear her

My phone vibrates.

I check my texts, expecting to see something from Joe or Anthony (who I'm still mad at).

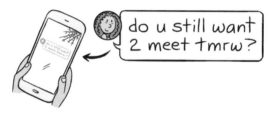

do u still want 2 meet tmrw?

I freeze. Does she know?

Guess not.

I don't respond. My mind is all jumbled up, and I can't think about tomorrow or anything else until I find out who posted that meme.

Except . . .

My face gets all hot again.

I can't think. That stupid meme!

The worst part is . . .

. . . after seeing it, I don't know if I can even look at Emmie again.

THE BOY goes to school. He thinks about the attic all day.

When he gets home, he sets up an experiment:

Then he leaves everything alone that night and goes to sleep.

Cont'd... zzz?...

Emmie

Later...

(Cont'd........)

TYLER

It was Ethan and Malik.

Being dumb. Playing a stupid joke. They weren't trying to be malicious.*

But they **were**:

stupid

hurtful

more damaging than the fire Kyle Duncan set in the chemistry lab last year

foosh!

WHEN YOUR EX HAS A GLOW-DOWN

Joe got it out of them. They apologized and deleted the meme, but not before half the school saw it or shared it.

*Winn Word

I don't know if Emmie saw it. I really, really hope not. I feel bad about blowing her off in those texts, but there's no way I can face her.

more embarrassed than when I dreamed I wet my pants in the cafeteria

Still, I guess I could've handled it better.

LeBron James

Not cool, little man.

I think about doing something distracting: homework, drawing my comic, playing Fortnite, practicing my trumpet, getting a snack (or five), listening to music, or going on SnabGab.

I do nothing.

I just sit here and feel bad.

I finally decide to go down to the kitchen.

This is one of the few times in months that Zach's said more than a couple words to me.

So much for that.

He begins heading downstairs. But I suddenly have something to ask. And he's in a good mood, so . . .

I think about how to phrase this.

Well, say Eli and Jonathan thought she was too dorky or something, and hassled you about it?

Wouldn't you do it? If they were just looking out for you?

Zach just stares at me.

Okay, first, I'm not friends with those guys to be cool. We're friends 'cause we've been tight since sixth grade.

An' second, if they didn't want _me_ to be friends with someone, I'd tell them off.

If they didn't listen, I wouldn't hang out with them anymore.

Even though you've been friends with them the longest?

Look, I don't know who this girl is, but if she's fun and nice and you like hanging out with her, then your friends should be good with that. Right?

Otherwise, they're not real friends.

Middle school.

He starts to leave but stops.

Guitar.

What?

Oh yeah, and coolness in middle school doesn't matter in high school.

If you wanna be friends with this girl, then do it. Who cares about everyone else?

He heads downstairs.

And I'm left staring after him.

It's the first time I realize that Zach's popularity isn't 'cause of "status."

It's 'cause he has something that I've kinda lost . . .

Winn Word of the Week

CONFIDENCE

Emmie

RECAP:

hey. sorry, can't meet. forgot i had a thing with my mom.

also mab we should just do our own comics. they wrk by themsvs.

new outfit = early birthday gift from parents (Bri's idea)

I FEEL LIKE I GOT STABBED IN THE CHEST.

RIP

"Here lies Emmie's heart"

285

I'M SO STUPID. I SHOULD'VE KNOWN. ESPECIALLY AFTER WHAT HAPPENED AT THE GAME.

I SIT. AND CRY. FOR A LONG TIME.

call me!

whoevr first posted took it down

so did most others. mab felt bad.

bink
bink
bink
bink

CALL ME!!!

HERE'S THE WEIRD THING: THE WORST PART ISN'T WHAT IT SAID ABOUT ME (BAD ENOUGH)...

sniff

...IT'S THAT IT REMINDS ME OF WHAT I'VE BEEN DOING TO SARAH.

TYLER

Monday morning.

ski goggles

Anthony in full
winter gear

SLOSH

I laugh, even though I feel like garbage.

or garbage's garbage

We leave it at that. One good thing about both Anthony and me: we don't hold grudges. Ever.

missing grudge glands

me   Anthony

I see Emmie walking to the restroom and I look away.

I stop. It's true. Anthony never said anything bad about her.

I sock him on the arm jokingly. It feels good that we're okay again. But . . . it isn't enough.

I know what I need to do.

Not only does **THE BOY** now
believe in ghosts...

Emmie

302

I HEAD TO HOMEROOM, EVERY-
ONE WHISPERING AROUND ME.

heart still
pounding →

stomach squeezy

BUT
head
up

I DON'T CARE.
I DON'T EVEN LOOK FOR TYLER.

THE GIRL tries to stay away, but the attic is too interesting.

WOOOSH

She only goes when the boy is gone. She doesn't want to frighten him...

oops

GAHH

...and she loves to take her time...

(cont'd)

TYLER

Whoa. Emmie did something really . . .

. . . un-Emmie-like.

Of course she thought that. Joe likes to tease her, probably 'cause she's quiet and he loves to get a reaction. He does the same thing with Sarah. She's not as quiet, but he's even worse with her. I've seen it.

The late bell rings. We hustle to get to homeroom.

As I walk into homeroom, something dawns on me.

Nah.

Emmie

317

TYLER

Emmie stands there, staring at me like I'm a cross between garbage and a slug.

It's the first time she's looked at me this way. Usually, it's:

I reach in my backpack and pull out a thick folder.

What's that?

My comic. It's almost done.

Tyler R. (private!) (no peeking)

'Cept some idiot wanted me to finish it by myself, and I realize that was the worst suggestion ever.

Especially 'cause I have the chance to work with the best artist in the school.

I hand her the folder and she takes it silently.

Is that, like, an apology.

Yeah. I'm sorry I was a jerk. And sent those texts.

Emmie still doesn't say anything, but she opens the folder and starts flipping through my drawings. I'm suddenly nervous, 'cause I worked really hard on the last batch. I spent all day Sunday finishing them.

I hold my breath.

For a long time.

turning blue

They're really good.

I release my breath.

Yeah?

Yeah. I like the detail in the attic. And the cross-hatching here.

320

Thanks. I think I spent an hour just on that section.

And you drew more butt clouds here.

I laugh and she smiles . . . just a little.

I know we have to talk about something else. Something I really **don't** want to talk about.

Listen, that meme...

She goes full-on Flamin' Cheetos. I think I do, too.

I say it quickly.

It wasn't Joe.

At first Emmie looks confused. Like she's trying to solve the world's hardest math problem.

Joe + something Joe would do [evil deed] = not Joe?

does not compute

Then who?

Just some idiots on the team. I told 'em off.

Told off Joe, too. For other stuff.

Emmie doesn't say anything.

Emmie looks at me, and I swear she's about to—

We stare at each other awkwardly for a moment.

Emmie

You have a private SnapGab message from a SnapPal

TYLER

It's freezing out. Not looking forward to that bus ride home.

Anthony nods.

He starts to spit and stops. I think his ex, Nikki Lourde, has

influenced him in her subtle way.

He doesn't say anything.

I think about my dad and his (and everyone else's) expectations about b-ball and grades and stuff. And my own.

Maybe changing those expectations isn't the worst thing. Maybe even benching it for a game or two wouldn't be the worst, either.

I just wanna stop all the pressure I'm putting on myself and go back to **enjoying** basketball . . . like art.

(sigh) I get it.

I'll still get back to practice and playing Fortnite and stuff.

Promise.

I'll hold you to it.

We split up. He heads down to the gym and I head out the door, when . . .

I hurry to catch up.

There's something I've gotta ask him.

Emmie

My roommate drove up for her dad's birthday, so I hopped along.

Light homework weekend.

You look cute. New outfit?

I BREAK DOWN AND TELL HER ABOUT THE PROJECT AND TYLER.

The funny thing?

I still like Tyler an' all...

TYLER

Everyone and their brother are here at the Student Showcase. Even my **own** brother. I thought my mom forced him to come, but weirdly, he seems to want to be here. We just walked through all the other arts and academic showcases.

Baked Bean
Girl ⤹

Poetry
Showcase

I proudly lead my mom and Zach to our comic book, which sits on a long table with everyone else's. People are allowed to look through.

I think we have a good chance at the prize. I'm no longer wishing for that as much as **some** people, but still.

←hopeful crazy eyes

Ms. Laurie will be here soon. She's going to announce the winners for best comic (by grade). Meanwhile, Anthony, Joe, Jaime, Maya, and a few other kids come to look at ours. Emmie's friend Brianna is here, too. Guess she won the science award.

twirl

But everyone's waiting around awkwardly, 'cause Zach (to my shock) is leafing through our comic book, appearing to read every single word.

Emmie looks like she might faint. She never met Zach, but she knows he's really popular and a basketball star. Also, he's not bad-looking.

Meanwhile, my mom—who doesn't get out much—is clearly enjoying being around other adults.

Emmie's parents and older sister are here. I don't know Trina, but Emmie's told me about both siblings. They're usually away at college, so she always feels like an only child. Makes me kinda glad Zach's still around, even if he's busy.

But here's the thing.

He's been different lately. He's still busy, but he takes more time to ask me about school and stuff and even promised to come to one of our practices next week.

Plus he's **here**, which is something. Or maybe he just likes the ego trip.

still drooling

Ms. Laurie finally arrives to announce the winners. She's holding the mystery envelopes.

also trying to hold gooey bake sale snacks

Suddenly, I'm kinda nervous.

clap clap
clap

For sixth grade, the winner is: Sophie Mendelson!

A tiny sixth grader with a long braid excitedly takes the envelope and thanks Ms. Laurie. She tears it open before she even gets back to her parents.

clap
clap
clap

Art supplies gift card!

secretly hoped for Taystee's gift card

I glance at Emmie, who looks like she's ready to tackle that girl for her prize.

Ms. Laurie clears her throat.

It's now my pleasure to announce the winner for seventh grade.

The winner is...

...Sarah Reyes!

My stomach drops with disappointment.

SQUEAL

Anthony gives me a consoling nudge.

My mom squeezes my shoulder and Zach says, "Tough break, Ty."

While Ms. Laurie announces the eighth-grade prize, I cross the hall to Emmie. She's alone. Bri is at the water fountain and Emmie's family is checking out the art.

And I mean it. For some reason, losing doesn't bother me that much.

She smiles, and something unexpected happens.

Whoa. What was **that**?

She goes to talk to her parents and Brianna.

Joe wanders over.

I nod at someone across the hall.

It dawns on him. He looks like he'd rather get kicked in the head by a yeti. But he gulps once and crosses the hall.

She stares at Joe, probably wondering what decent spirit took over his body.

355

They keep talking. I notice they're the exact same height.

I had thought about how Joe kept trying to get Sarah's attention. And how it was different from the way he usually acted. It was almost like he kept trying to . . . compliment her or something. In his twisted Joe way.

I finally got it out of him.

Surprising, since they seem so opposite. But crushes are unpredictable.

I hold up my hand. Emmie high-fives mine.

Ms. Laurie walks over, nibbling a brownie. I think that's her fourth one. The woman can really put 'em away.

Hi, guys. Well done! I wanted to let you know it was really close.

You should be pleased with your project. Good teamwork.

We tell her we are.

Consolation prize! I got these from the cupcake table. Shh, don't tell the others.

We laugh as she hands us a secret stash of mini cupcakes. Then she joins some parents.

I feel my phone buzz in my back pocket. I check. It's my dad on FaceTime. I'm kinda surprised and excited he remembered the Showcase.

I walk around the corner to a quieter hall.

My heart sinks. He forgot.

I groan to myself. I know it was just a question. And I no longer care that we didn't win. But he didn't even remember what it was that could win. That "it" was a comic book. And that I teamed up with Emmie. And that I worked my butt off for weeks.

But I try to let it slide.

Hi, Tyler! Sorry, I need your dad's help with our enchiladas! He'll have to say goodbye!

Unbelievable.

It can wait, 'Chelle. I'd like to talk to Ty.

But—

It can wait.

I can't believe he finally stood up to her.

(grumble) Fine, I'll start them myself.

Sorry you didn't win, Ty. But I'd love to see your project when I visit.

I cheer up instantly. That was not what I expected.

We talk a minute longer until I hear my name called. Mom.

I realize everyone is waiting.

(not so patiently)

My drooling reflex kicks in at the thought of a double-fudge
brownie sundae. Nice of Ms. Laurie, but those teeny cupcakes
didn't cut it.

Also not what I expected. I know there's an ulterior motive of
shake and SUV privileges, but still.

We head through the front door. I look at everyone and think:

But sometimes . . .

. . . weird feels just right.

EPILOGUE

They do this all week.

Z Z z^ZZ

wiped by end of week

To their amazement, they realize they have a lot in common.

So you like art, too?

Yes. I was pretty good when I was alive.

≈STOP≈ ≈PLAY≈

You're good now.

You too.

≈STOP≈ ≈PLAY≈

Did you have any pets?

A dog, Agnes.*

≈STOP≈ ≈PLAY≈

I have a dog, Snoopy.

My favorite comic strip!

(* after the painter, Agnes Martin)

They become friends.

One night, **THE BOY** invites his (human) friends to the attic to "meet" The Girl.

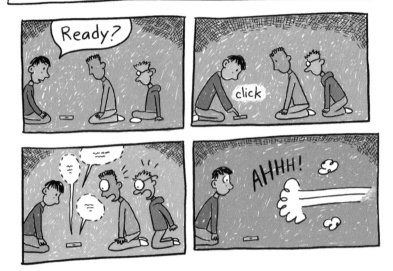

It seems like no one approves.

FROM THE CHILDHOOD ARCHIVES OF TERRI LIBENSON

Kindergarten

Seventh grade

ACKNOWLEDGMENTS

I wrote (and rewrote) Tyler during the Covid-19 pandemic of 2020. Admittedly, it was a struggle. Between having "quarantine (aka sluggish) brain," writing from a boy's viewpoint (gasp), and dealing with a rambunctious new puppy (see photo)—let's just say my recycling bin was overflowing. Ironically, I had retired my syndicated comic strip and its daily deadlines, yet for the first time I found myself stressed about getting this book finished on time!

Luckily, it all came together in the end, and it turned out better than I imagined. I was able to write authentically, eke out a story I loved, and even managed to create a book within a book. It couldn't have happened without the following people:

Donna Bray, my amazing and knowledgeable editor, whose phone conversations held me together.

Dan Lazar, my supersupportive agent, who also encouraged me like no other.

Laura Mock, Amy Ryan, Jon Howard, Vanessa Nuttry, Mitch Thorpe, Vaishali Nayak, Tiara Kittrell, and the rest of the team at HarperCollins, who are incredibly talented, kind, and tireless. You guys had a challenging year but made everything seamless.

Michael, my supportive and long-suffering husband, who has come to terms with the fact that I live in my office.

My kids, Mollie and Nikki—also long-suffering but wonderfully adaptable. Thank you for caring for the fur baby during these weird times.

Aaron, who I know is up there, still happily peddling my books to friends and strangers.

Amy and Mina, who kept me sane with our back-and-forth messages and memes. I needed that levity!

And of course, my readers, who send me the best letters, pictures, messages, and emails. I may not always be able to write back, but I **always** love hearing from you!

pandemic pup Rosie (summer, 2020)